W9-BNY-651

Tree-House Comix Proudly Presents
DOG MAN
Twenty Thousand Fleas Under the Sea
WRITTEN AND ILLUSTRATED BY DAV PILKEY
AS GEORGE BEARD AND HAROLD HUTCHINS
WITH COLOR BY JOSE GARIBALDI & WES DZIOBA
graphix
AN IMPRINT OF
SCHOLASTIC

Library of Congress Control Number 2022944016

978-1-338-80191-0 (POB)
978-1-338-80192-7 (Library)

10 9 8 7 6 5 4 3 2 1 23 24 25 26 27

Printed in the U.S.A. 61
First edition, March 2023

Editorial team: Ken Geist and Jonah Newman
Book design by Dav Pilkey and Phil Falco
Color by Jose Garibaldi and Wes Dzioba
Color flatting by Aaron Polk and Corey Barba
Creative Director: Phil Falco
Publisher: David Saylor

CHAPTERS
chief

DOG MAN: He's part dog, part man, and ALL HERO! Sometimes he dresses up as a superhero named "The Bark Knight," although he has no superpowers.

PETEY: He used to be an irritable, impatient bad guy. But when his son arrived, Petey became determined to change his ways. Now he's an irritable, impatient Good Guy.

LI'L PETEY: Petey's pure-hearted son. He loves making comics and telling Jokes. Sometimes he even saves the world as a superhero named "Cat Kid."

MOLLY: She may *look* like a tadpole, but she identifies as a baby frog. Her superpower is *psychokinesis*, which means that she can move things with her mind.

SARAH HATOFF & ZUZU: Sarah is an investigative Journalist from Australia who adores her pet poodle, Zuzu. Sarah always carries a purse, too, except when Harold forgets to draw it.

CHIEF: He's Dog Man's brave boss and loyal best friend. Chief also has a HUGE CRUSH on Nurse Lady. Don't tell anybody!!!

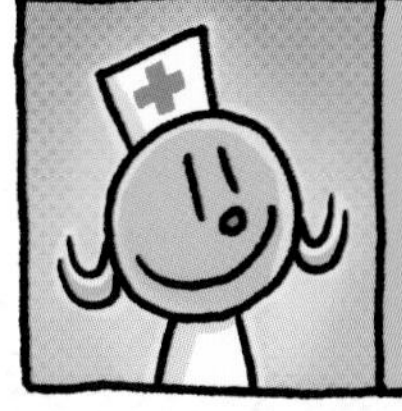

NURSE LADY (a.k.a. Genie S. Lady, RN, BSN): She's a smart and brave health-care professional, and her quick thinking saved Dog Man's life. She also has a MAJOR CRUSH on Chief. Shhh!!!!

80-HD: A robot designed by Petey and rebuilt by Li'l Petey. Although his exoskeleton houses a limitless supply of helpful gadgets, his greatest superpower is CREATIVITY.

PIGGY: He's the ruthless leader of the FLEAS, which is an acronym for "Fuzzy Little Evil Animal Squad." Recently, Piggy got shrunk by a shrink ray, and was locked up in Mini Jail for "crimes and stuff."

CRUNKY & BUB: Piggy's sidekicks and members of the FLEAS. Crunky (the gorilla) and Bub (the crocodile) also got shrunk and locked up in Mini Jail, but unlike Piggy, they're both pretty good guys.

DARYL: He's a friendly moth who founded a superhero club called "The Friendly Friends." Daryl is a loyal friend to Piggy, even though Piggy is mean and rude in return.

For my brother,
Steve Aragaki

CHAPTER 1
DOG MAN JUMPS THE SHARK

chief
We're almost there!
chief
Thanks for coming with me on my date, DoG Man!!!
chief
I'm a little **nervous!**
chief
Is my breath okay?
chief
sniff sniff

chief
chief
Oh, boy! This is Gonna be...
chief
...GREAT! She's already HERE!!!
chief
SHARK SHACK

What do I DO, Dog Man?
What do I SAY?
chief
What if she doesn't LIKE me anymore???
chief
chief
Push
push
Push
chief

PUSH
PUSH
PUSH
PUSH
SHARK
chief
HiYa, Chief!
Umm--- h-h-hi,
Nurse Lady.
And Hello,
DoG Man!
SLURP

chief
chief
chief
chief
Well...
chief
...Gee...
chief
...Um...
chief

chief
Tap
tap
Tap
chief
chief
Oh!
Do You like the sky?
chief
Yeah, I Guess so.
chief
Oh.
chief
chief

SHARK SHACK
chief
WELL?
chief
ARE YOU THREE BLABBER-MOUTHS GONNA ORDER SOME FOOD????
HEY!!!
WHAT'S THAT DOG DOING HERE??

He's not a DOG.
He's DOG MAN!
Chief
Well he Looks Like a DOG to ME!!!
AND WE don't ALLOW DOGS!
Oh, Yeah? Well I don't see a SIGN!!!

chief
NO
NO
DOGS
NO
DOGS
ALLowed

NO DOGS ALLowed
Are You happy now?
NO DOGS ALLowed
chief
And Since You've VIOLATED our SIGN...
NO DOGS ALLowed
chief
... I'm Gonna Take this DOG LEASH...
CLick

...and tie him to this TRASH CAN where he belongs!
chief
Now he can't cause ANY TROUBLE!!!
HAW HAW HAW!!!
HAW HAW HAW HAW
HAW HAW
zip

H-HEY!!!
ZOOM
YAAAAAAAAAAAAAAAAAA
CRASH!

SMASHY
KLUNKA
ZOOMIES
FLOOSHUMZZZ
SHAR
FONZARELLI

ZZZZZiP
GOTCHA
SPLACHULA
DRIP
DRIP
DRIP
DRIP
DRIP
UNCLICK
WHOOOOSH

You better not hurt him!!!
Who's Gonna STOP Me???
We ARe!!!
With the Power of FLiP-O-RAMA!
INTRODUCING
FLiP
Cheesy Animation Technology

STEP 1.
First, Place your Left hand inside the dotted Lines marked "Left hand here." HoLd The book open FLAT!
STEP 2:
Grasp the right-hand Page with your Thumb and index finger (inside the dotted Lines marked "Right Thumb Here").
STEP 3:
Now QUICKLy fLip the right-hand page back and forth until the Picture appears to be Animated.
(for extra fun, try adding your own sound-effects!)
RAMA
...FOR A BoLd, New WorLd

You can't tell me what to do!
Oh, yes we...
chief
...CAN!
chief
You and what ARMY?
Him and this FOOTY!!!
chief
Let the fight begin
Left hand here.

Date Fight

Right
Thumb
here.

Date Fight

And so...
Are You okay, Dog Man?
chief
chief
Welp, I Guess We better Go!!!
chief
Okay! But first...

POP
TWIST
TWIST
NO DOGS ALLOWED
chief
NO DOGS ALLOWED
NO DOGS ALLOWED

NO
DOGS
ALLowed
NOW
DOGS
ALLowed
NOW
DOGS
ALLowed
That's better!
Chief
NOW
DOGS
ALLowed
Oh, Look! New Customers!!!
Chief
RUFF
RUFF
RUFF
RUFF
RUFF
RUFF
RUFF
RUFF
RUFF
RUFF RUFF
RUFF RUFF

How sweet!!!
chief
See ya later, Sunshine!!!
chief
chief
What's wrong, Chief?
Chief

This date was a DISASTER!
Are You Kidding?
This WAS the Funnest DATE EVER!!!
chief
Thanks, Chief!!!
Hi-5

By George Beard and Harold Hutchins

Meanwhile...
You MUST Be this SHORT to Enter.
MiNi JaiL
MiNi JaiL
Oh, hi, PiggY!

TODAY'S Lunch
PIZZA, GRITS, CUPCAKES
How's it Going?
Did You Guys get my Secret escape plans?
Yyyyeah...
Well? Did You STUDY Them??
Well... ummm...

W-W-We don't wanna escape from Mini Jail, Piggy!!!
WHAT? This is MADNESS!!!
But we like it here, Piggy!
Yeah! We like working in the cafeteria!!!
Look at the yummy cupcakes we baked!

Wanna try one?
NO, I DON'T WANNA TRY A CUPCAKE!!!
I'm Not even Hungry Anymore!
You Guys Made me Lose My Appetite!!
How Could You Be so SELFiSH???

MOVE OVER!
NOM
Nom
Nom
Nom
Hey, Piggy, can I have one of your
NO!
I ONLY HAVE Seven Left!

Do You WANT me to STARVE To DeATh?
no.
SELFiSH!!!
Hey, Piggy! You've got a Visitor!!!
DARYL!!!
IT'S About Time!!!

HEY!!!
38259
SWIPE
38259
PEEL
FLING
74449

SMUNCH
SMUNCH
VISITING
ROOM

Soon...
Hiya, Piggy!
Piggy
Well? Did you bring it???
Aren't you even going to say hello?
Hello, DARYL! Did you bring the CANNERY GROW?
No!

NO??? WHY NOT?
They don't make it anymore. The factory was destroyed!!!
But I brought you something even BETTER!
Piggy
SWIPE
Piggy
CRINKLE
CRINKLE
CRINKLE
PIGGY
PIGGY
What's THIS?
PIGGY

It's your COSTUME!!!
Piggy
COSTUME?? What For?
Piggy
For our CLUB, Piggy!!!
Piggy
Don't you remember the Friendly Friends?
SLap!
I Just recruited TWO New Members!

And I figured, if we're Gonna be Superheroes...
...We're Gonna need COSTUMES!
These are the MOST RIDICULOUS COSTUMES I've EVER Seen!
They Look Like BABY CLOTHES!!!
WHO Would be DUMB Enough To wear Something Like THIS?

Hiya, PiGGY!!!
'Sup?
PLOP
Aw, Look! We touched PiGGY's heart!!!
With FRiendLY POWER!!!
WAAAAAA

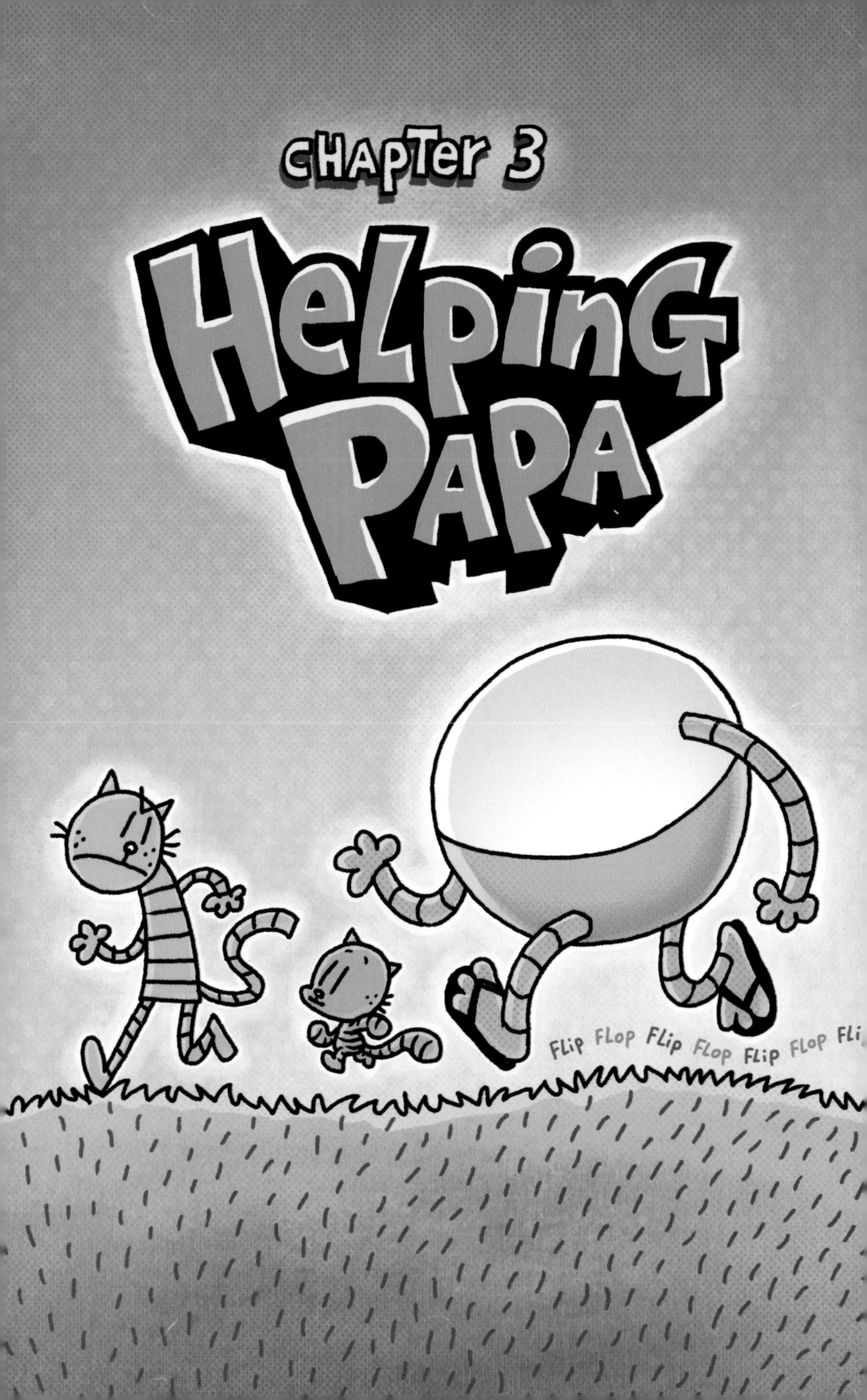
CHAPTER 3
HELPING PAPA
FLIP FLOP FLIP FLOP FLIP FLOP

ALRIGHT, we've Got a LOT of WORK to do...
FLIP FLOP FLIP FLOP FLIP FLOP FLIP
...So I don't want You two PLAYING!!!
Why?
Because we've Got to REBUILD our LAB!!!
Why?

Because I need a place to Live!!!
Why?
Because I can't keep living at Dog Man's house!
Why?
FLIP FLOP
FLIP FLOP
FLIP FLOP
BECAUSE YOU GUYS ARE SOOOO IRRITATING!!!
Why?

Because You're NOISY...
...You're MESSY...
... And You think everything is SOOOO HILARIOUS!!!
Why?
Because You—
CUT THAT OUT!
Why?

ARE YOU JUST GOING to be A WISE GUY ALL DAY???
Yeah, Probably.
WELL, That's JUST GREAT!
You PROMISED to be GOOD TODAY!!!
You BEGGED to come with me!!!
You SWORE to be helpful!!!

But we haven't even STARTED...
... And You're ALREADY being A BIG PAIN!!!
I'm sorry, Papa.
This is NOT PLAY-Time!
Do You hear me?
You Are NOT here to PLAY!

And that Goes for YOU, TOO!
NO PLAYING!
NO PLAYING!
NO PLAYING!

Hi, Guys!
Do You want to play?
OKay!
Let's GO!
FLip FLop FLip FLop FLip FLoP FLip FLop FLip FLop FLiP

Meanwhile...
GRRRRR
GRUNT!!!
UGHRRR
PUFF
PUFF
PUFF
PUFF
PLUP
PLUP
It's No Use!
I CAN'T GET THIS RIDICULOUS SHIRT OFF!

I think PiGGY needs our HELP!!!
How about a FRiendLY Friend HUG?
SQUiSH
Awww!!!
How SWEET!!!

SQUASH
Let Go
OF Me!

IF You Three BUG BRAINS want to HELP...
...then Get my ESCAPE PLANS...
...STUDY them...
...And...
BOOM
...And...
BOOM

WHOA!
WHAT'S HAPPENING?
BOOM
It's An EARTHQUAKE!!!
BOOM
BOOM

The WALLS ARE CRUMBLING!
We're ALL GONNA Die!
Bye-Bye, Crunky!!!
So Long, Bub!!!
WHAT COULD Be CAUSING this UNFATHOMABLE CALAMITY?

Chapter 4
Bad Mister Stinkles
Mini Jail
You must be this short to enter.

Hey!!!
That's A BAD Mister Stinkles!
You put that down RIGHT NOW!
Drop it...
DROP it...
STINKLE RAMA
Left hand here.

...YOU Drop that MAXimum Security CoRRectional FACiLity RiGht NOW!!!

Right Thumb here.

...YOU DROP THAT MAXIMUM SECURITY CORRECTIONAL FACILITY **RIGHT NOW!!!**

MiNi Jail
MiNi Jail
MiNi Jail
Sniff
Sniff

KRACK
FLIP
Pat
Pat
Pat
Munch
Munch
Munch
Good Mister Stinkles!!!

Well...

...Come on, Crunky!!!
WHERE ARE YOU TWO GOING?
We're Gonna find Your Secret Plans...
...and figure out how to ESCAPE!

OKay, DarYL—
Let's Go!!!
But, PiGGY...
...What about Crunky and Bub???
FORGet About Those GuYS!
They're SO SELFiSH!

ALL They CARE About is HELPING OTHERS!
They NEVER PUT ME FIRST!
But we can't Just leave them behind!
OH, SO YOU'RE SELFISH, TOO, huh?
IT'S ALL ABOUT YOU, isn't it???

I'm--- I'm sorry, Piggy!
Less cryin', more flyin'!!!
O-O-Okay, Piggy.
FLAP FLAP
Hey!
Wait for us!!!
So long, suckers!!!
Boo Hoo Hoo

CHAPTER 5
A BUNCHA STUFF THAT HAPPENED NEXT
Chief

Meanwhile...
chief
Hey, Look! It's a SWING!
chief
Let's swing on it!!!
Gee whiz. Do You think it's SAFE?
chief
Of course it's safe...
chief
CHOMP-O-RAMA
Left hand here.

...what could **POSSIBLY** Go **WRONG?**

Right Thumb here.

...what could **POSSIBLY** Go **WRONG?**

chew
chew
chew
chief
SNAP
chief
BUMPA
DUMPA
chief
BOMPY
GROMPY
chief
BLUMPITY
KLUMPITY
STUMPITY
chief
FLOMP!

I'm — I'm sorry, Nurse Lady.
chief
I'm sorry, too.
chief
Sorry we didn't try that SOONER!
chief
Let's DO it AGAiN!!!
chief
C'mon, fellas!
chief
chief

Meanwhile...
DONNA'S CONSTRUCTION
OK, Mr. TheCat...
I'll help You rebuild Your lab.
Let's Get Started!
CTion
Hey, look! There he is!!!
FLip FLop FLip FLop FLip

Hi, Wally!!!
Guess what we did?
Molly, I don't
We made You a Present!
See?
It's a comic about YOU!!!
Oh, how sweet!

Look, I apprecia
Your breath Smells like coffee.
I APPRECIATE YOUR GIFT...
...But I DON'T have Time to READ it RIGHT NOW!!!
That's okay, Wally!
I'LL read it FOR You!!!
SLAP!

WALLY'S WORLD
BY MOLLY and Li'L Petey
COLOR BY 80-HD

One time Wally was in a BAD MOOD.
as USUAL!
First, he slipped on a ba-nana peel...
ZIP
Then he fell down the stairs...
...Then a bee stung his butt.
I'm MAD!
So I'm gonna build my own world...

...where nobody can Bother me!!!
Bam Bam Bam
So Wally Started Building.
Bam Bam
He worked...
Bam
...and worked.
Bam Bam Bam
Finally, he was done.
Paint
Paint

Buh Bye!!!...
Wally Floated to Outer Space.
Now I can Be happy!!!
But then...

Well? Did ya like it, Wally?
NO!!!
It doesn't even make SENSE!
And why was the last part BLANK?
Oh. We couldn't think of an ending.
Or a middle.

Sometimes it's hard to think up ideas!
Yeah.
Oh, I see...
...So if something is REALLY HARD...
...You Just QUIT?
Is that right???

Is THIS what You teach in That COMIC CLUB of Yours???
no.
no.
IT'S TOO HARD...
...So let's Just Give UP!!!
Because we're ALL A bunch of Little baby...
...QUITTERS!

We're sorry, Wally.
AND MY NAME'S NOT WALLY!
It's PETEY!
PETEY!!!
PETEY THE CAT!

Wait– YOU'RE Petey the Cat?
Yeah.
Aren't you the guy who stole all of those toilets...
...And made everybody wet their pants???
Um... that–
–That was a LONG TIME AGO.

I've already been Punished for that!
I paid my Debt to Society!
AND the Governor PARDONED me!
Ever since then, I've lived my–
Hey! Where are You Going???
AWAY FROM YOU!
But YOU SAid You'd help me Rebuild my LAb!

You're on your own, Jailbird!!!
FLIP FLOP
FLIP FLOP FLIP
Don't worry, Wally.
We'll find somebody else to help you!!!

Meanwhile...
WAAAAAA
WAAAAAA
I CAN'T believe They LeFt without us!!!
It's SO SAD!!!
But then...
WAAAAA
Hey, Ducky— What's that noise???
WAA

Beats me, Mike!
WAA
Let's find out!!!
WAAAA
Hey, Look! It's Crunky And Bub!!!
WAAAAAAAAAA
And they're CRYING!
Should we help them?
Okay!

And So...
WAAAAAAA
We're helping YOU CRY!
Thanks, Ducky!
If only You could help us FLY!!!
We can do that!
FWOOSH
FWOOSH!

CHAPTER 6
FRIENDLY FRIENDS ARE GO!

Meanwhile...
Aaah- Freedom at Last!!!
But I miss Crunky and Bub!
Would You Forget About those Guys?
They're Nothing But TROUBLE!!!
ALL they do is EAT, LAUGH...
...And make up RIDICULOUS SONGS!!!

And FURTHERMORE...
HIYA, PIGGY!!
We're BAAAACK!!!
We Just made up a NEW SONG!
Do You wanna hear it?
NOOOOOOOOOOOOOOO!!!
and a one, and a Two, and a...

Note: This song can be sung to the tune of "Jingle Bells."

Friendly Friends,
Friendly Friends...
...Armed with
Friendly Hugs...
...OH, What Fun
it is to Ride...
...on the BACKS of
Friendly Bugs!
DASHING Through
The SKY...
...on a beetle,
moth, and FLY...

...O'er the hills so high...
...Laughing till we cry!
HA! HA! WAA!
Soaring through the air...
...Swooping here and there...
...What fun it is to share and care...

...Without our underwear!!!
WOULD YOU CUT THAT OUT??!!
We've Got A Serious Problem Down There!
What's wrong, Piggy???

SHHHHHHHHH!!!
chief
It's that DOG-Headed Cop!!!
He's Sound Asleep, So Don't make Any Noise!!!
What?
GROWL-O-RAMA
Left hand here.

GRR-FACE A GO-GO!

Right Thumb here.

GRR-FACE A GO-GO!

RUFF RUFF RUFF RUFF RUFF
Watch out, Daryl! We're Gonna CRASH!!!
RUFF RUFF RUFF
The BEACH
Supa-Sized SUBS
$5.99
No, we're not!!!
The BEACH

Uncle Larry!
DARYL!!!

What IS this Place?
It's the FriendLY Friends Action HeADQUARTERS!
We can use this technoloGY...
... to spread Joy and Sunshine ALL over the WORLd!
Yeeeah...
... that's EXACTLY What I was thinkinG!

CHAPTER 7
CAT CELL CULTURE

Meanwhile...
Sorry. I can't help you.
HELPFUL HOME REPAIRS
ALWAYS OPEN BUILDERS
Sorry. We're closed.
Sorry, but I lost my tools...
NO CO

...and my hand hurts...
...and it's too sunny...
No excuses construction
FLIP FLOP FLIP FLOP FLIP FLOP
...and my truck won't start...
FLIP FLOP FLIP
How come nobody will help us?

Because I went to Jail...
...and I- HEY!
I told You this story in the LAST BOOK!
Oh.
Oh.
We Probably weren't listening.
Yeah! Tell us AGAIN!

What's the Point???
I TRY to DO GOOD!
I TRY and I TRY...
... but nobody cares.
I'll ALWAYS be the bad guy.

Meanwhile...
RUFF RUFF RUFF RU
That sounds like DoG Man!!!
RUFF RUFF RUFF RUFF RUF
COMe on, ZUZU!
What's **WRONG**, DoG Man?
The BEACH
SUPA-Sized SUBS

Something's up at The Beach?
UNDER their roof?
Under the...
...under the "C"?
Umm... is it ITCHY?
Is it fleas?

It's Fleas?
Are You talking about PiGGY and his Pals?
THE FLEAS ARE BACK???
And there are MORE of them?
OH, NO!!!
I better alert the Media!!!

Beep Boop Boop
Beep Boop
The Media
Ring
Ring
Hi, Sarah. What's up?
News Desk
Bob!!! Listen closely!!
The FLEAS ARE BACK!!!
...And there are MORE of them than EVER!!!

They're at The Beach under the "C."
At the beach? Under the sea?
NEWS DESK
Yeah. It's where they make those Supa-Sized Subs!
They're MAKING SUBS?
OH, NO!!!
click
I better tell the Boss!!!
NEWS DESK

BOSS
Two minutes Later...
SUPA-Sized SUBMARines?
Yeah! And there are MORE than EVER!!!
That's A SWELL SCOOP!!!
BuT we GoTTA Punch it up!!!
Give it some MOXie!!!

HOW MANY MORE ARE There?
Gee whiz, Boss. I don't Know.
It could be one... Ten... A hundred...
... a Thousand... or even TWENTY Thousand!
TWENTY THOUSAND?
That's Your HEADLINE!!!
ZONG
BOSS

Twenty THOUSAND FLEAS UNDER The SEA!!!
Now Go Write me A Story I CAN Sink my CHOPPERS Into!!!
BAM
OKay, but...
BOSS
...those Numbers might not be true.

TRUE?
TRUE?
NOBODY CARES About The TRUTH!
This is the NEWS, Baby!
It's ALL About the CLicKS!!!
BOSS

CHAPTER 8

The Media Network
BREAKING NEWS
TWENTY THOUSAND FLEAS UNDER THE THE SEA
GET PAID TO CLICK ON ADS!!! EASY CA$H!
I made nine cents!
Advertisement
DEATH SUB FOR PIGGY
Photo Collage Illustration
INVASION ALERT!!!
Sponsored
ANONYMOUS AUTHORITIES FEAR DOOMSDAY
Does Piggy plan to DESTROY our way of of life with his BLOODTHRISTY, KILLER SUBS?
Click here to learn how YOU can SAVE YOUR way of life for only $19.99 per month. Act NOW!!!
FARTS
I ♥ FARTS
I ♥ FARTS
FARTS
Paid Actors
SUPA FLEA SPRAY
Not a real doctor.
Advertisement
JOIN THE "FLEAS ARE REALLY TERRIBLE SOCIETY" TODAY!
Click here to resell "FLEAS ARE REALLY TERRIBLE SOCIETY" (FARTS) Merchandise.
Click here to save on "FLEAS ARE REALLY TERRIBLE SOCIETY" Tattoo Removals.
Sponsored
Warning: Do not use around pets or humans. May cause horrifying side-effects.
DOCTORS RECOMMMEND NEW "SUPA FLEA SPRAY"
Click here to save 10% on SUPA FLEA SPRAY side-effects remedies.
Click here to save 5% on remedy for side-effects of SUPA FLEA SPRAY side-effect remedies.

Meanwhile...
This place is AMAZiNG!!!
Thanks, PiGGY! MY Uncle Larry built it all.
He's a Genius!
AW, Shucks!!!
And what is THAT?
Oh, that? It's a FLYinG Sub!

I was inspired by the f
Nobody cares!
The only thing I care about is...
...Does it WORK?
It sure does!
Oh, boy! Oh, boy! Oh, boy!!!
It's ALL I EVer WANTED!!!

It's BEAUTIFUL!
And the BEST PART is...
I've Got the WHOLE PLACE to MYSELF!!!

ALL ABOARD!!!
HEY! GET OUT OF HERE!!!!
OKAY, PIGGY! Let's Get this sub out of here!!!
FOOOSH
FOOOSH
But WAIT! We can't fit through that TINY DOOR!!!
SUB SUB SUB

Don't worry, Piggy...
...Watch this!!!
Size -O- TRON
SUPA DOOPA BIG
SUPA BIG
BIG
NORMAL
SMALL
SUPA SMALL
SUPA DOOPA SMALL
Our built-in Size-O-Tron can make this sub SHRink!!!
KA-KLUNK
Size -O- TRON
SUPA DOOPA BIG
SUPA BIG
BIG
NORMAL
SMALL
SUPA SMALL
SUPA DOOPA SMALL

SUB WILL SHRINK IN FIVE SECONDS...

...FOUR...

...THREE...

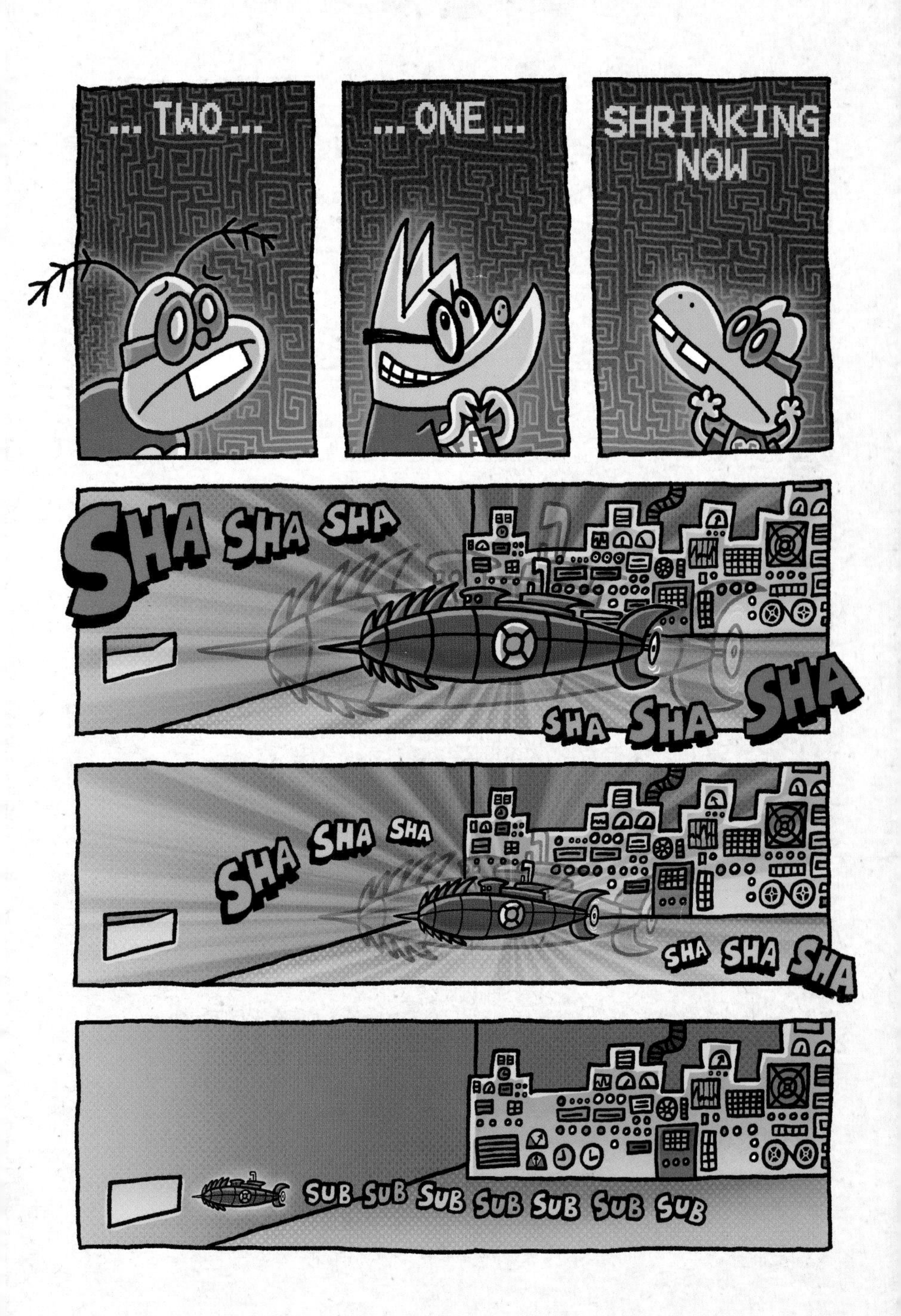
...TWO...
...ONE...
SHRINKING NOW
SHA SHA SHA
SHA SHA SHA
SHA SHA SHA
SHA SHA SHA
SUB SUB SUB SUB SUB SUB SUB

And so...
BEACH
SUB SUB SUB SUB SUB SUB SUB
SUPA-Sized SUBS
$5.99
Nice Job, Uncle Larry!!!
Aw, shucks!
Now can you make us Grow SUPA BiG?
I sure can!!!
Size -o- TRON
SUPA DOOPA BiG
SUPA BiG
BiG
NORMAL
SMALL
SMALL
KA KLUNK
SUB WILL GROW IN FIVE SECONDS...

But then...
Hey!!!
This story isn't TRUE!
TWENTY THOUSAND FLEAS UNDER THE THE SEA
I Never SAID TWENTY THOUSAND!
I Never SAID there were SUBMARINES!
SUBMARINE ALERT
SHA SHA SHA
I Never...
SHA SHA SHA
...never...

SHA SHA SHA
The BEACH
SUPA-Sized
SUBS
$5.99
Umm...
...Never mind.

CHAPTER 9

FOLLOW THAT SUB

We interrupt this story with a TERRIFYING Report!
The MEDIA
All across the beach...
...Protesters have Gathered to oppose TWENTY THOUSAND FLEAS...
Fight the FLEAS
FLEAS
Dehydrate the Sea!
Lock Him up!
...Who are hiding Under the SEA.
UNDER
Experts believe these Fleas...
Unidentified Expert

...Could ATTACK at ANY MOMENT!
RAR!
And So, our World TREMBLES in TERROR!
Excellent!
The Whole World is AFRAID!!!
But we're the Friendly Friends!
We want to make everyone HAPPY!

We ARE Going to make everyone happy!!!
But HOW?
Well? What makes YOU Guys happy?
Laughing!!!
Playing!!!
Smiling!!!
Cupcakes!!!
Those are ALL Good Answers...
...If you're Five years old!!!

But Some folks are more COMPLEX!
Some folks need COMPLEX things to make them happy.
Like what?
FEAR and ANGER!!!
Fear and Anger make people happy?
They sure Do!!!
Boop

Fear and Anger Trigger Dopamine Receptors in the Brain...
I ♡ Dopamine®
...And That makes People Happy!
We've Already Scared them...
STOP THE SUBS
FLEAS GO HOME
Now we need to make them MAD!
But HOW?

OH, there are so MANY, MANY WONDERFUL WAYS...
Politics...
...inflation...
...Social Media...
SUB SUB SUB SUB SUB

OR, we could throw pies at People!
Where did You Get those???
From the Pie-MAKinG MAChine in our Kitchen!!!
Pies! Pies! Pies! Pies!

Chapter 10
PIE FIGHT
SPLAT
FREEZE THE FLEAS

ALRiGht, if we're Going to thRow Pies at People...
...we HAVe to do it RiGHT!
So there will be No GiGGling...
...NO TOM-FOOLERY...
...And MOST IMPORTANTLY...
...NO SinGinG!
And a ONe, and a Two, and a...

NOOOOOOOOOOOOOOOOOOOOOOO
Friendly Friends, Friendly Friends, Flying through a cloud...
...We made up a second verse...
...and we'll sing it SUPA LOU-UD!
Friendly Friends, Friendly Friends...
...Cozy, cute, and clean...

...Oh, What fun it is to Ride...
...in a FLYING Submarine!
DASHING Through the Skies...
...on a Submarine that fLies...

...Dropping Pumpkin Pies...
...on Some Random Guys!!!
PLOP
PLOP
PLOP
Making People MAD...
...is the opposite of BAD...

...So Spread some cheer with RAGE and fear...
...And Then You'll be so Glad!!!
YOU...
...GUYS...
...ARE MAKING ME...

...SO ANGRY!!!
OH, BOY!
That means we're making PIGGY HAPPY!
I KNOW!
Let's SING it 153 MORE TIMES!!!
NOOO

Friendly Friends,
Friendly Friends...
Um... hello.
What are you all doing?
nothin'.

Well, the whole world needs your help...
...So Let's GO!!!
No thanks.
Nobody wants to help US...
...Why should we help them?
What's Going on Here???

Well, everybody hates my Papa.
Yeah, and they'll Probably hate us, too...
...if **We** ever make a mistake.
So **We're** not taking **ANY More Chances!**
Oh, I see.

So...
...if Somebody Gives You a hard time...
...You Just QUIT?
Is that right?
Is THAT the way a HERO acts?
No.
No.

OOH- People CAN be MEAN!!!
So Let's Just Give UP...
...because We're ALL a bunch of Little BABY...
...Quitters!!!

We're Sorry, Sarah.
You're darn right You're **Sorry**!
NOW Get up off of those butts...
... And Let's GO SAVE the WORLD!

And so...

FLiP FLOP FLiP FLOP FLiP

Sarah is the SMARTEST PERSON EVER!
I Know!
HEY!!!
I SAID THE SAME THING a few CHAPTERS ago!!!
Yeah...
...but it Sounded better when She said it.

CHAPTER 11
PIGGY MAKES HIS MOVE
FF

Well, folks, We're back at the beach...
...where FEAR has turned to OUTRAGE!!!
FLeas Go Home
SPLAT!
A MASSive Pie FiGht has begun...
... and Citizens are Getting HUFFieR AND PUFFieR!!!
Peace
YOU'LL PAY FOR That!!!

But I didn't throw that Pie!
Well, it didn't Just fall out of the SKY!
Good Point!
Authorities fear that everybody's OUTRAGE...
Anonymous Authority
...may cause them to Lose Focus...
What's-his-face
... on the REAL ISSUE!
Which is?
Umm... I forgot!
SPLOP!

But then...
FOOOOOSH
SUB SUB SUB
SHHHHHHH
HI-
YAH

FREEZE, FLEAS!!!
Fleas?
Who are the Fleas?
Fleas?
38259

Wait—Aren't You Guys The FLEAS?
No.
We're the Friendly Friends!
Oh. Umm...
...Are we on the right Submarine?
Well, we USED to be "The Fleas"...

...but then we chan
I DON'T believe MY LUCK!!!
EverYbodY I CAN'T STAND...
...is TOGether in ONE PLACE!
Now's my Chance...
...To DESTROY THEM ALL!!!
SIZE-O-TRON
SUPA DOOPA BIG
SUPA BIG
BIG
NORMAL
SMALL
SUPA SMALL
SUPA DOOPA SMALL

SIZE -O- TRON
SUPA DOOPA BIG
SUPA BIG
BIG
NORMAL
SMALL
SUPA SMALL
SUPA DOOPA SMALL
SUPA DOOPA POOPA SMALL
Okay, now you're just being silly.
KA-KLUNK
SUB WILL SHRINK IN FIVE SECONDS...
SNAP
...FOUR...
... THREE ...
... TWO ...

...ONE...
SLAM
SHRINKING NOW
SHA SHA SHA
SHA SHA SHA
SHA SHA SHA
SHA SHA SHA
SHA SHA SHA
SHA SHA SHA
SHA SHA SHA
SHA SHA SHA

All of my Problems...
...are Getting smaller and smaller!!!
SHA SHA SHA
SHA SHA SHA
Bye-bye, **Losers!**
SHA SHA SHA
I think I'll send them all off...
SHA SHA SHA
...with a STANDING OVATION!
SLAP-O-RAMA
Let's Get PiGGY WiTH it!
Left hand here.

C'mon, Get SLAPPY!
Right Thumb here.

C'mon, Get SLAPPY!

Well, that was...
...
...HEY!!!
Where ARE they?
scratch
scratch
scratch
Oh, well...
...it's CRIME TIME!!!

Chapter 12
ZOOM IN

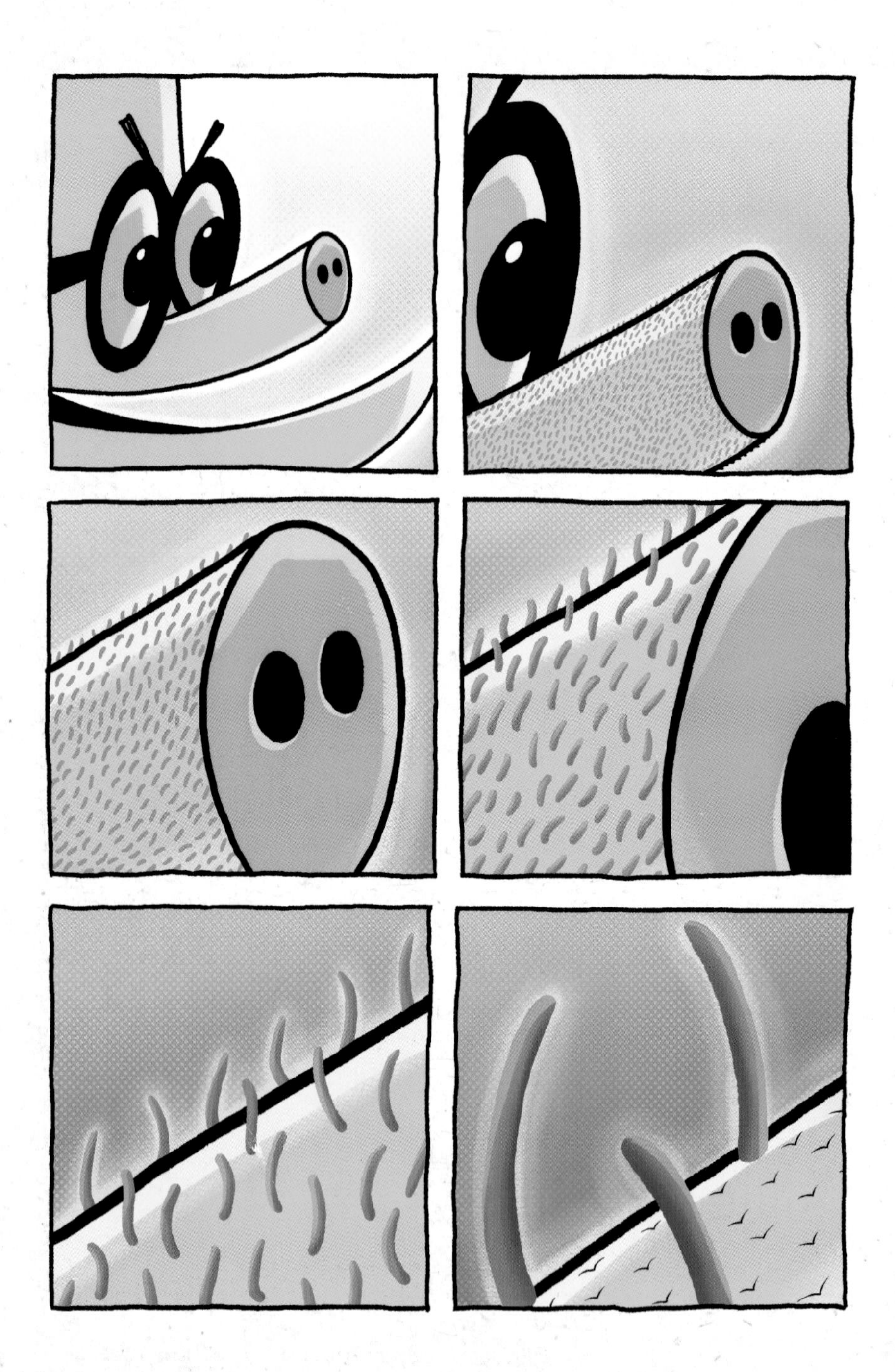

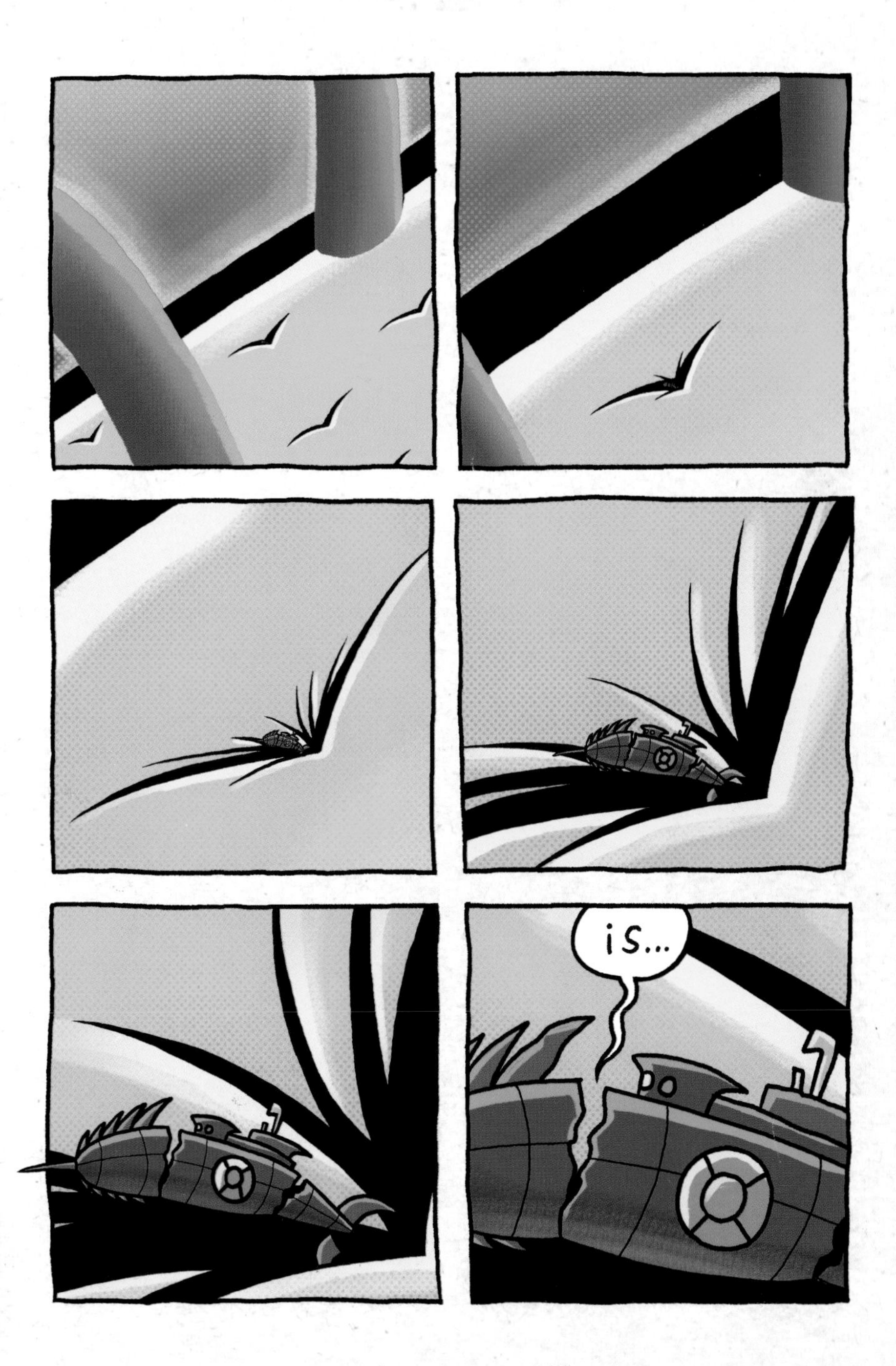
is...

...is everybody okay?
Yeah, I think so.
WHAT happened?
It appears we've SHRUNK to MICROSCOPIC SIZE!!!
Status Report
You Small!!!

Our sub was DAMAGED...
...we've lost our PROPELLER...
RRRRRRRReeeeeeeeT
...AND WE'RE SLIDING INTO A SWEAT GLAND!!!
SSSSSSLIP

Let's Just Grow BiG AGAin!!!
We CAN't!
OUR Size-o-TRon is BUSTeD!!!
Well, Goodbye, Bub!
So Long, Crunky!
YAAAAAAAAAAAAAAAAAAAA

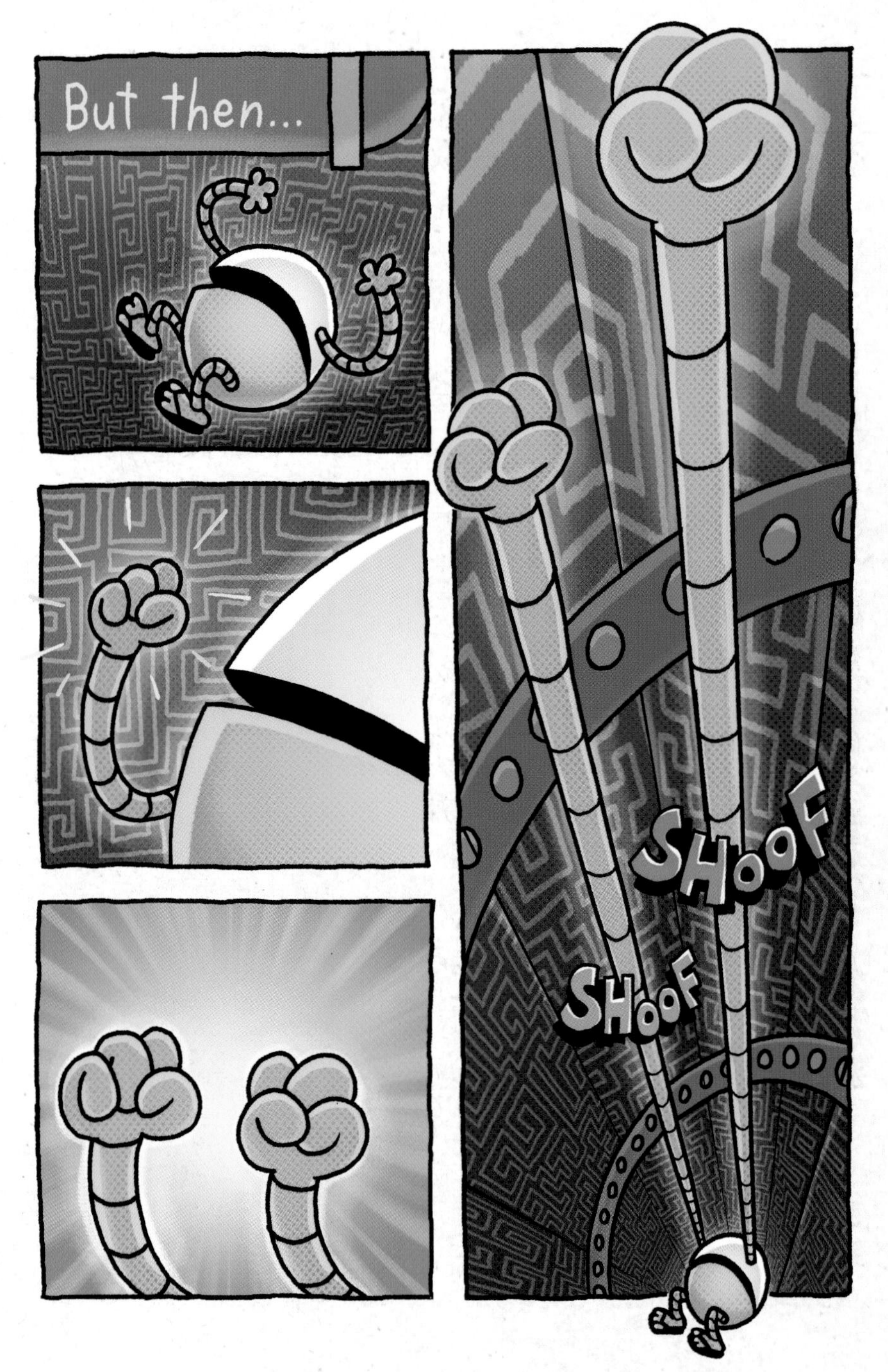
But then...
SHOOF
SHOOF

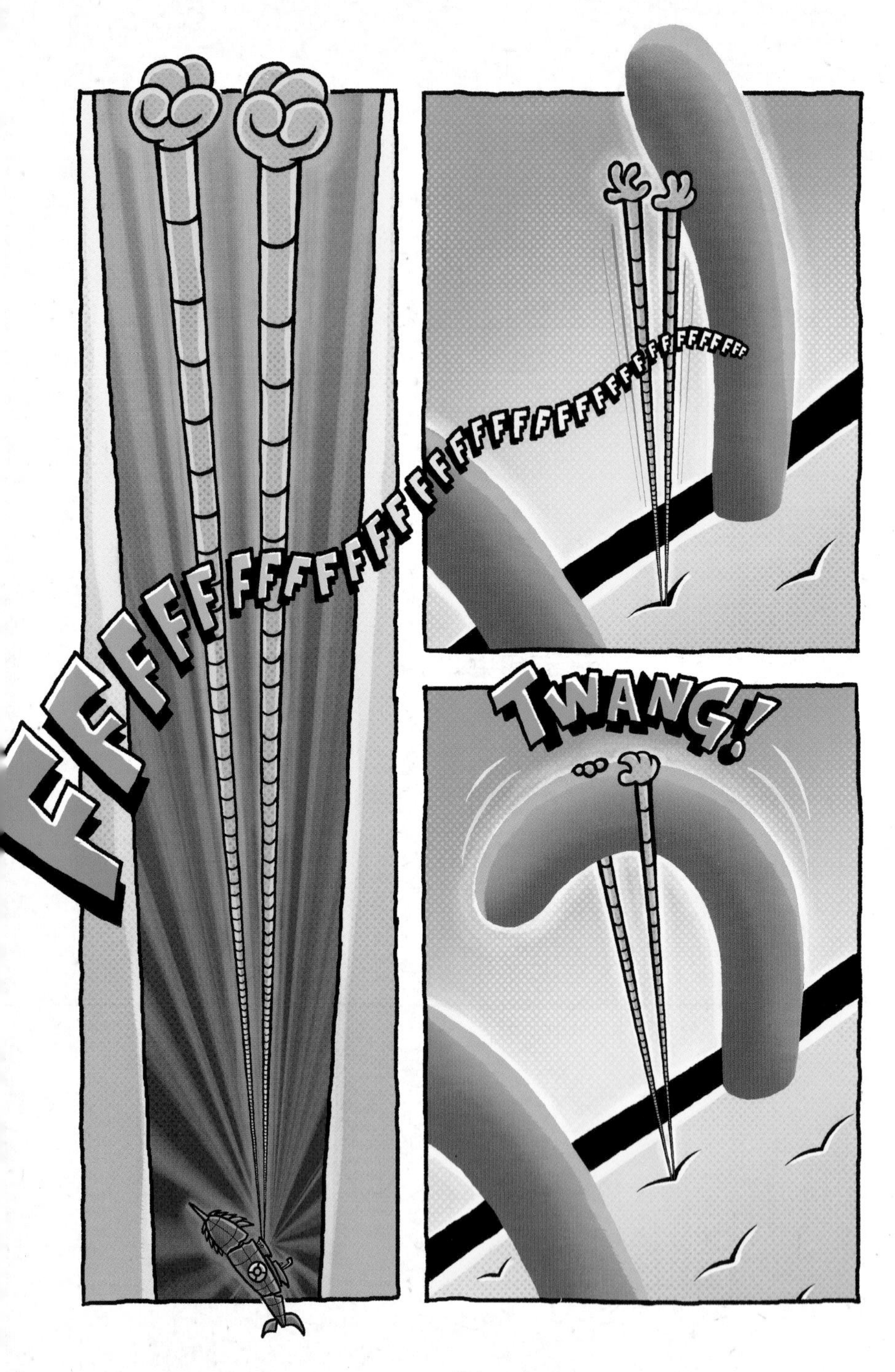
FFFFFFFFFFFFFFFFFFFFFFFFFFFFFFFFFFFFFFFFFFFFFFFF
TWANG!

80-HD SAVED US!!!
HOORAY for 80-HD!
We're not out of this yet...
You in BIG trouble, brah.

We need Someone to dive into the ABYSS...
Beach Balls
SNORKLES
DIVING GOGGLES
... and fetch our PROPELLER!
Somebody who's not afraid to Get Stinky!!!
Do We have any Voluntee—
SWISH!!

Hey, DoG MAn! WAit UP!!!
PLOP
PLiP
PLeeP
Now it's time to Fix this Sub!
Aye, Aye, CAPTAin!

The three brave friends swam DOWN...
... and brought the Propeller back UP!
But then...

CHAPTER 13
THIS MITE BE A PROBLEM

The propeller was recovered...
... and reattached...
SSSSSSSSSSSSSSSSSSSSSSSSSS
This is Glue. Strong Stuff!

...and soon the damaged Sub...
SUPA DOOPA BIG
SUPA BIG
BIG
NORMAL
SMALL
SUPA SMALL
SUPA DOOPA SMALL
SUPA DOOPA POOPA SMALL
This is tape. Strong Stuff!
...was set to soar again!!!
This is acrylic Latex caulk. Strong Stuff!
I think we're ready to Go!!!
What could Possibly Go wrong???

But then...
RAAAR!!!
Help! It's A Giant Monster!
Actually, it's really just a Microscopic Parasitic Mite...

...of the Genus: **Demodex**.
In small numbers, they're quite harmless!
UNCLE LARRY!
This looks like a job for the SUPA BUDDIES!

We need our COSTUMES!!!
COSTUMES
And so...

Something is MissinG!
Hey...
What about 80-HD??
Oh, yeah!
Hey, we need HELP!!!
Would you HURRY UP?
COSTUMES

WE ARE HURRY UPPING!
You Guys can't be the SUPA Buddies...
COSTUMES
... if You don't Got 80-HD!!!
She's right! 80-HD's hands are FULL!
Maybe I can take his place.
But You don't have a costume!

ZONG
FWOOSH!
zip
zip
KA-SHONK

ZONG
ZONG
ZING
ZING
snip snip
snip
FLOOOSH
ZUZZA
ZUZZA
WHAT'S TAKING SO LONG???

We're doing Something IMPORTANT! Gee Whiz!!!
And so...
I look AWESOME!
Thanks, 80-HD!
Now we Just need to think up my SuperHero NAME!

AW, COME ON!!!
SERIOUSLY?
OKAY, OKAY!!! Jeez Louise!
We can work on my Superhero name after we...
...HEY! Where did everybody GO?

You're too late, Kid!
GRRR!
Be nice, Zuzu!!!
I think everybody Got SWALLOWED!
HEY!!!
You Let GO OF OUR FRiENDS!

HAW HAW HAW HAW HAW
CHOMP
Let's Get him!
FLIP-O-RAMA
BASH THAT BUG!
Left hand here.

Mitey Fighty

Right Thumb here.

Mitey Fighty

BOING!
ZIP
GRAB
RAR
GLUB
SLURP

CHAPTER 14
AND THEN THERE WERE TWO

I'm Scared, Bub!!!
Me too!
I thought FEAR was supposed to make everybody HAPPY!
It's Not Working!!!
But then...
Hey!

Wait a minute.
It's not JUST Fear...
...it's ANGER, too!
Oh, Yeah!!!
But how do we—
Pies!!!

Kitchen
ZiP
HAW HAW HAW
SPLAT

WIPEY WIPEY WIPEY
FLICKITY-FLING
SPLAT
SPLAT
SPLAT
Tee Hee
Hee Hee
Tee Hee
Hee Hee Hee

But then...
Taste
Taste
Taste
NOM?
SSSLLLUURRRRRRRP!
NOM NOM!

Oh, So You Like these Pies, huh?
They're Pretty GOOD, aren't they?
Well, PARK Your Ponies, Junior!
THERE will be NO MORE Pies FOR YOU...
...Unless...

...You Give us back OUR Friends!!!
RAAAR!
Don't You TALK BACK to Me!
WHO Do You THINK You ARe?
THIS is MY HOUSE!!!

AND I WANT MY FRiENDS BACK!!!
GLAAAL
SPLOP!

Come Get Your Pies, Junior!!!
KICK
ZOOM
NOM NOM
NOM NOM!

SPLASH
Let's Get OUT oF Here!!!
OKAY! START The EnGines...
AYe, AYe, CAPTAin!
Start
CLICK
...Reel in those ARMS, 80-HD...
ZiZZZZLe
FOOOOSH
FOOOOSH
...And Get Ready to GROW!!!
KA-KLUNK
Size -O- TRON
SUPA DOOPA BIG
SUPA BIG
BIG
NORMAL
SMALL
SUPA SMALL
SUPA DOOPA SMALL

Hey, Uncle Larry?
Yes?
Can we Grow **SUPA DOOPA BiG?**
Gosh! We've never Tried **ThAT** before!
Size -O- TRON
Let's do it!!!
KA-KLUNK
Size -O- TRON
SUPA DOOPA BiG
SUPA BiG
BiG
NORMAL
SMALL
SUPA SMALL
SUB WILL GROW IN FIVE SECONDS...
...FOUR...

CHAPTER 15
EXACTLY ONE HUNDRED AND NINE SECONDS EARLIER

Well, THAT was easy!!!
I robbed Five banks today...
... and nobody even NOTICED!
They're All too busy being SCARED and ANGRY!!!
Beach
Nobody is Paying Attention to the REAL Problem...
... which is ME!!!

Now it's time to RELAX in my LUXURIOUS NEW CASTLE...
PIGWARTS
...Which I Just Purchased with my ILL-Gotten GAins!!!
PIGWARTS
Aah—This is the Life!
Root Beer
What could Possibly Go Wrong?

But then...
SHA
SHA SHA
SHA SHA
SHA
SHA SHA SHA
SHA SHA SHA
SHA SHA SHA
ROOT BEER

SHA
SHA
SHA
ROOT BEER
CRASH
CRASH
SHA
SHA
SHA
SHA
SHA
SHA
PIG WARTS
SMASHUMS

MY...
MY...
...MY ILL-GOTTEN GAINS!!!
WAAAAA
WAAAAA
WAAAAAAAAAAAAA
WAAAAAAAA
PIG
WARTS

WAAAAAAAAA
CLOP!
Wow!!! Look how Little Piggy is!!!
Aww— He's SO CUTE!!!
Can we keep him?

If You Promise to make him HAPPY!
Oh, we Know how to do THAT!!!
HEY! NO SinGinG!!!
And a one, and a TWO, and a...
Friendly Friends, Friendly Friends...

...FLYING 'CROSS THE PAGE...

PIGGY IS OUR LITTLE PET...
Shoehorns
BACK Scratchers
Piano Benches
FONDUE POTS
HAMSTER CAGES
Umbrella stands

...AND HE LOVES HIS LITTLE CA-AGE...

Friendly Friends, Friendly Friends...
Guinea Pig Food
...watch him eat his meal...
...OH, what fun...
...to see him run...
...on a friendly hamster wheel!!!
WAAAAAAAAA

Chapter 16
In Search of the Depth

KA-KLUNK
SIZE -O- TRON
SUPA DOOPA BIG
SUPA BIG
BIG
NORMAL
SMALL
SUPA SMALL
SHA SHA SHA
And in the end, old friends...
...new friends...

...and friends we sort of forgot about ten chapters ago...
chief
COSTUMES
...all worked together...
chief
FLIP FLOP FLIP
NAILS
PAINT
...to help Petey rebuild his lab.

Soon, it was time to stop for the day.
chief
Let's all Go to Dog Man's house!
We can eat supper together!
HOORAY!!!
And so...

Thanks for all of your **Kindness**, everyone.
I told you we'd find somebody to help you, Wally!
But...
... but why Me?
That's why we're here, Papa...
... to help each other.

It's like the sea, Petey...
You can just dip your toes in...
...or you can FATHOM the Soundless Depths.

That's what I was talking about...
...back in Chapter 5!!!
You can do the BARE Minimum...
...and SLIDE through life...
...or You can Give MORE...
...Give what YOU didn't Get...

...LOVE MORE...
...And DRop the OLd STORY!!!
THAT was my WHOLE POINT!!!
Yeah, we Know...
...but it ALWAYS sounds better when SHE says it!!!
FLOP FLip FLap FLiP FLOP FLip FLOP

The
chief
FLIP
FLOP
FLIP
FLOP
FLIP

End

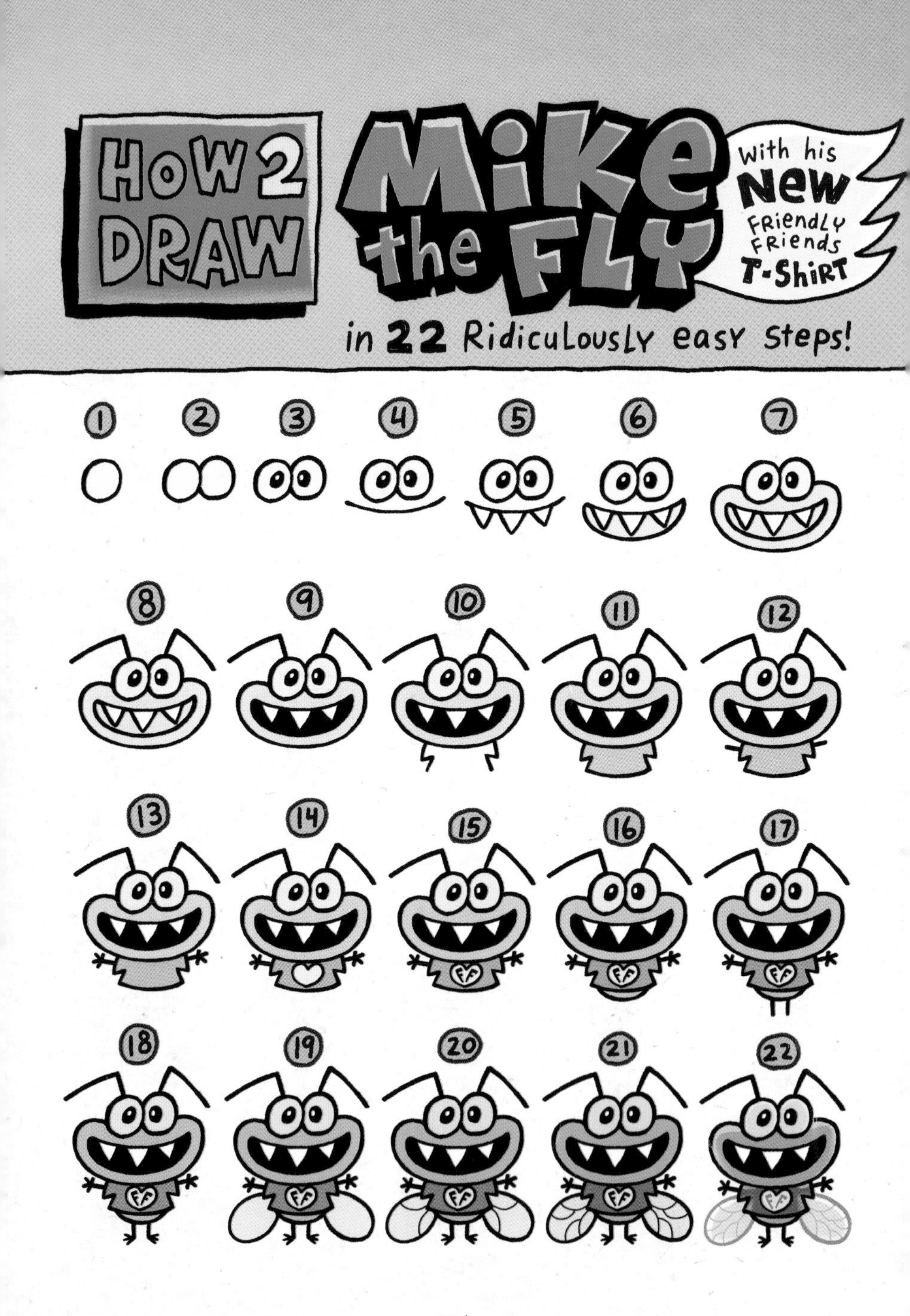
HOW 2 DRAW
MIKE the FLY
With his NEW FRIENDLY FRIENDS T-SHIRT
in 22 RIDICULOUSLY easy steps!
1
2
3
4
5
6
7
8
9
10
11
12
13
14
15
16
17
18
19
20
21
22

HOW 2 DRAW
MOLLY
WHO STILL hasn't figured out her SUPERhero name Yet!!!
in 16 Ridiculously easy steps!
1
2
3
4
5
6
7
8
9
10
11
12
13
14
15
16
FOR MORE "HOW 2 DRAW" Fun...
PLANET PILKEY
...VISIT PLANETPILKEY.COM
PLANET PILKEY

GET READING W

THE INTERNATIONAL BESTSELLER
DOG MAN
DAV PILKEY
CREATOR OF CAPTAIN UNDERPANTS
DOG MAN UNLEASHED
DAV PILKEY
DOG MAN A Tale of Two Kitties
DAV PILKEY
DOG MAN AND CAT KID
DAV PILKEY
DOG MAN LORD OF THE FLEAS
DAV PILKEY
DOG MAN BRAWL of the WILD
DAV PILKEY
DOG MAN FOR WHOM THE BALL ROLLS
DAV PILKEY
DOG MAN FETCH-22
DAV PILKEY
DOG MAN GRIME AND PUNISHMENT
DAV PILKEY
DOG MAN MOTHERING HEIGHTS
DAV PILKEY

FROM THE CREATOR OF DOG MAN
CAT KID COMIC CLUB
WRITTEN & ILLUSTRATED BY DAV PILKEY
A GRAPHIC NOVEL FROM THE CREATOR OF DOG MAN
CAT KID COMIC CLUB PERSPECTIVES
WRITTEN & ILLUSTRATED BY DAV PILKEY
A GRAPHIC NOVEL FROM THE CREATOR OF DOG MAN
CAT KID COMIC CLUB ON PURPOSE
WRITTEN & ILLUSTRATED BY DAV PILKEY
A GRAPHIC NOVEL FROM THE CREATOR OF DOG MAN
CAT KID COMIC CLUB COLLABORATIONS
WRITTEN & ILLUSTRATED BY DAV PILKEY
★"Irreverent, laugh-out-loud funny, and . . . downright moving."
— Publishers Weekly, starred review
MY DOG
SUPA FAIL
Monster Cheese Sandwich